Loving Someone Is Not Enough

A Love Story

Love can be perfect… but still not survive. This is a story about finding your most perfect partner, and losing them — not because the love failed, but because the world around it made staying impossible.

Written by Jason Alan

First Edition

ISBN: 979-8-234-03551-6

Published by Jason Alan Inc.

Rights and permissions inquiries:
Jason Alan Inc.

Printed in the United States of America

This book is based on personal experiences and reflections. Certain names, details, and identifying characteristics have been changed to protect the privacy of individuals.

Dedication

To Betty Anna — a woman God sent into my life to say goodbye on behalf of a grandmother I never got to properly let go of.
She taught me that loving someone is not always enough — but that it's still always worth it.

She brought me back to love.

To Our Spiritual Advisors — the ones who saw us coming before we ever met.

To Those Who Whispered Truth from Behind the Veil, who reminded us that love is real, even if it's not always easy.
That faith connects souls long before eyes ever meet.

To God.
To Family.
To What Truly Matters,

LOVE.

My Most Perfect Partner

(Written January 3rd, 2024)

25–36 years old.

5'2–5'8.

Black/brown hair.

Skinny. 120lbs–130lbs.

Dark eyes.

No race.

Christian/Catholic/Christ-like.

College degree/higher/willing to learn.

Unmarried/single/no children.

Open to life partnership pending marriage.

No one that needs to be fixed.

Athletic. Exotic looking.

Good career.

Someone who is stable.

By 6/5/24.

Author's Note:

A Love Beyond Boundaries

It came to me, somewhere along the way, that this story is more than just a love story. It is a calling. A deeper understanding of faith, humanity, and the kind of love that exists when two people choose to see each other fully — not in spite of their differences, but because of them.

As a Christian, I never imagined that my path would lead me to fall in love with a Muslim woman. And yet, she entered my life not as a coincidence, but as something — or someone — placed by God to challenge, teach, and open my heart.

This story is about two people from different worlds. Different faiths, cultures, and families. And yet, despite it all — or perhaps because of it all — we found love. A love rooted in mutual respect, shared values, and a fierce commitment to honoring one another's beliefs.

In a world so often divided by religion, politics, and fear, I believe this story carries something sacred. It is proof that love can grow from the most unlikely places. That peace can start between two people who choose understanding over assumption. That respect — deep, honest respect — can build a bridge stronger than we ever imagined.

We didn't try to change each other. We listened. We learned. We believed — in our own ways, and in something greater that brought us together. And even though the love didn't last forever in the form we had hoped, its impact was eternal.

This book is for anyone who has questioned whether love can overcome barriers. It can. It did. And through it, I came to see that God doesn't always give us what we expect — He gives us what we need to grow.

What you're about to read is a journey of two hearts, two faiths, and one truth:
Love, real love, doesn't care where you come from. It cares who you are.

Table of Contents

The Message

"You are my most perfect partner."

There are some messages you don't delete — not because you're holding on, but because you already know you'll never feel something like that again.

This story started with an apartment rental. A name. A click. A phone call. Then a knock on a door, not knowing that opening it would change everything.

She wasn't just another client. She became my teacher, my mirror, my love, my best friend, my most perfect partner.

This is the story of how we met, loved, lost — and why sometimes, love really isn't enough.

Part I: The Spark

The Showing

Anthony:

It started with a lead.
Just another apartment inquiry online — or so I thought.

"Amira, interested in an apartment on 7 Whitehouse St — can you show today?"
No photo. No background. Just a name and a phone number.

I called right away and left a message.
She didn't pick up.
About an hour later, she texted back — short, to the point.

"Hi, I can come today if that works."

She didn't waste words. There was something refreshingly direct about that. She wasn't chasing charm — just clarity. I told her I was more than sixty minutes away, but she was already eager to see it. So, I asked my partner, Alek, to meet her first. He's been in the business for decades. I figured he'd open the door — and I'd handle the rest.

When I arrived mid-showing, she was already walking the space.
Confident. Calm. Dressed in all black — like she was prepared for a business meeting, not just an apartment showing.

I stepped in, smiled, and introduced myself.
"Hi, I'm Anthony — we spoke earlier. I'm the one you're renting from."

She nodded but still called me "Alek." Twice.

We laughed about it later. It became our first inside joke — her calling me by my partner's name, and him looking nothing like me… just sharing a first letter.

She had questions. Specific ones.
Parking. Noise. Appliances. Ceiling height. Entry points.
At one point she asked me to go upstairs so she could see what it sounded like when walking across the floors.
I liked that. She was picky — and I respected that kind of intentionality.

"I'm not just going to take something because it's available," she said.
"I need to feel at peace where I live."

We wrapped up the showing, and she told me she'd think about it.
The next day, she texted again.

"Can I come by one more time? I'm deciding."

I met her again, this time showing her a second unit that had just opened on the top floor — a lucky break.

The first was slightly more affordable, but it had a bit of a history. An elderly woman had passed away in it just two months prior. I didn't tell her — legally I didn't have to unless asked and I still don't think she knows.

But the upstairs unit? Corner unit. Private. Quiet. No one above.
She paced it slowly, looked out the window. I could see it in her face — she was already imagining herself there.

Still, she hesitated.
"It's a little more than I wanted to spend," she said.
Then, without missing a beat:
"Will you reduce your commission if I sign?"

I smirked.
She was serious.

I told her if it was up to me, I would, but that I needed check with my partner—though I already knew the answer. Since I had a business partner, we both had to agree on any commission cuts. I was willing, but he wasn't, so it didn't happen this time.

She tried a few times. Negotiated. Pitched different angles.
It never worked, but I admired the effort.

Eventually, she agreed.
The upstairs unit was hers.

She signed the lease, but we still had one last step: collect the checks.

At the time, I thought I was just renting another apartment.
But I remember watching her walk back to her car — deliberate, focused, unreadable.
And something in me paused.

I didn't know her yet.
But I knew I wanted to.

And that's how it started.

***

Amira:

I was wearing all black — not because it was planned, but because black is easy. Safe. Professional. No room for mistakes.

I remember walking through that apartment with a checklist in my head: noise, light, distance from the neighbors, the stairs. I asked about the floors. Had him walk upstairs to test the sound.

He laughed. But he did it.

I didn't think he'd remember that moment. But later… he told me he did.

He told me I looked like I belonged there. I didn't feel like I did yet — not really. I was just trying to prove to myself that I could be on my own.

When I called him Alex — twice — I could tell I'd thrown him off. But he didn't correct me rudely. He smiled. Said "Actually, my name is Anthony."

And something in the way he said it made me stop.

I don't know why I asked to see the place again the next day. Maybe I needed another look at the apartment. Maybe I just wanted another look at him.

I didn't know he was watching me walk to my car.

And I didn't know, not yet, that the next time we met — he'd ask me for coffee. And everything would start to feel different.

Coffee & The Couch

I met her to collect the checks. That's when I casually asked if she wanted to grab a coffee — and unknowingly stepped into something bigger than paperwork.

There was a different energy to her this time. She was wearing all black, green sneakers and when I complimented her, she fired back right away:

"I'm dressed for war."

That line caught me off guard, and I laughed.
She had this way of mixing seriousness with humor— like she was letting you in, but only just a little.

The paperwork was easy. The small talk wasn't— it wasn't small at all. There was a kind of immediate comfort, but also a cautious distance. I could tell she was used to keeping her guard up. I didn't want her to feel like this was just another transaction.

So, I asked, "Want to grab a coffee while we're here?" She hesitated, but I could see the smile.

We went to that Starbucks, our first date.
I made fun of her for ordering something complicated, a green tea matcha with Oat milk and she teased me about being basic, an Americano.
We talked for hours about everything and nothing — families, growing up, the stress of moving, the weirdness of adulthood.
There was never an awkward silence. When there was a pause, it felt natural.

Later, she mentioned she still needed furniture.
I saw an opening: "Need help picking something out?"
She didn't say yes, but she didn't say no either.

So, off we went to the furniture store.

We walked into the store like a couple, even if we weren't one yet.
She'd flop onto a couch, judge it, then glance over at me for approval.
"I need a good plop," she said.

"I just want to see if I can handle living on my own," she joked. I teased her for her high standards. She shot back: "Better than settling."

I didn't realize at the time how much that line would echo.

We stood arguing about a ridiculously overpriced beige couch.
She loved it. I hated it.
The debate lasted at least ten minutes, not because the couch mattered, but because disagreeing felt easy and safe.

On the way out, I asked if she wanted to grab dinner.
She looked at the time and her mood shifted — not cold, just like something heavy had landed on her shoulders.

"I have to go," she said.

I tried to lighten it up: "Curfew?"
She laughed, and for the first time, the walls dropped just a little.
"Something like that," she said.

She walked to her car, glanced back just once — and that was it.

I stood in the parking lot longer than I needed to, feeling like I'd just lived through a chapter I'd want to reread someday.

I didn't know what was happening between us — but I knew it wasn't just about coffee or couches.
It felt like a beginning. Quiet. Unnamed. But real.

I went home that night replaying her jokes, her questions, even the way I corrected her about my name.
There was something here.
Something just starting to unfold.

And then, later that night, she texted me:
"You're dangerous."

I smiled.
I didn't know what I was walking into.
But I knew one thing —
I wanted to stay in it.

***

I wasn't planning to say yes. But when he asked if I wanted to grab coffee, something in me said: try.
It wasn't the coffee.
It was him.

He wasn't pushy. Just present.
And for someone like me — someone always calculating the risks — that mattered more than he knew.

I joked that I was "dressed for war."
He laughed like he didn't take it personally — and that surprised me.
So many men get uncomfortable around a strong woman with boundaries. He didn't flinch. He leaned in.

I didn't know then how much I needed someone who made space for both my sharpness and softness.
But I felt it.

I watched the way he looked at me — not just at me, but into me. Like he noticed the things I tried to keep tucked behind careful smiles and sarcasm.

At the furniture store, I played it cool — but when he followed me, gave honest opinions about couches, stood beside me without trying to take over... that's when I started to feel safe.

When I told him I had to leave, he didn't guilt me.
He made a joke and let me go.
That mattered too.

Later that night, I texted him:
"You're dangerous."
Because he was.

Not in the way men usually are.
He was dangerous because he saw me.
And I was starting to want to be seen.

Part II: The Rise

Becoming Her Safe Space

Moving day came quickly.

She didn't ask me for help.

But I showed up anyway.

There was no grand plan — just a couple of boxes, some scattered bags, and a look in her eyes that said, "I'm doing this, but it's not easy."

Amira had never lived alone before.

This wasn't just a move — it was a transition. A declaration. A quiet storm of independence and vulnerability mixed together in a one-bedroom apartment with good lighting.

I carried her nightstand up the stairs and offered to hang a few frames.

She laughed and said she didn't know where she wanted them yet.

"Start with one," I said. "Then the others will follow."

We weren't dating. We weren't even calling this anything.

But I was there — and she let me be.

Over the next few weeks, I became her unofficial moving consultant, tech support, handyman, and occasional lunch delivery guy.

One time, she texted me asking if I knew how to fix her Wi-Fi.

I was there within an hour, even though I knew she could have called the provider.

She just didn't want to feel alone.

Another night, she had trouble sleeping.
Too quiet, she said. Too much space for her thoughts.

So, I stayed on FaceTime with her until she fell asleep.
Didn't talk much. Just... existed with her in the silence.

She was building a life, and I was quietly becoming part of it.
Not because I was trying — but because she felt safe with me.

And I loved that.

There was no pressure. No titles.
Just two people, slowly learning how to show up for each other.

I noticed things — how she lined her shoes up perfectly, how she couldn't eat while standing, how she'd text me instead of call when something was really bothering her.

I never pried. But I never left her alone in the dark either.

She never said the words, but I felt it:
"Thank you for making this easier. Thank you for being here."

That apartment became her sanctuary.
And somehow, without either of us saying it, I had become part of that safety too.

It wasn't romance yet.
But it was trust.

And that's where real love starts.

***

I didn't ask him to come on those days.
I wanted to—but I didn't know how.
I'd always done everything myself, so moving alone felt natural. I carried more than I should have.
I didn't want to seem weak. I didn't want to need anyone.

But when I saw him walking toward me with my nightstand in his arms…
something in me exhaled.

I wasn't used to someone just showing up without needing to be asked.
Not out of obligation. Not because it was romantic.
Just because I was important enough to show up for.

He didn't try to fix everything.
He just offered. Stayed. Carried what he could — physically, emotionally.

The night I texted him about the Wi-Fi, I didn't really need help.
I just didn't want to feel alone in a space that still echoed.

And the night I couldn't sleep, he stayed on FaceTime — not talking, not asking.
Just… breathing next to me in the dark, even from far away.
That's what safety started to feel like.

I didn't say it out loud.
But I felt it — in the way I smiled when his name popped up,
In how my day shifted when I knew he was near.

I had moved into my own place.
But he was the first person who made it feel like home.

When Everything Felt Like Us

There wasn't a single moment that made it real.
No first kiss. No anniversary.
It was just one day I was dropping off her soup, and the next, I was texting her to rest and checking if she ate enough.

It happened slowly — like a routine that built itself.
She'd send short messages:
"Did you eat?"
"Get some rest."
"You're not sleeping enough."

I started doing little things for her — not to impress her, but because it felt right.
Lentil soup from her favorite restaurant.
Dropping sushi and frozen yogurt off at my door because she knew I was overwhelmed and probably hadn't eaten.

She never asked.
But she never pushed me away either.

Sometimes I'd text just to say I was thinking of her.
Other times, I'd show up with food and leave it outside — just to make her day a little easier.
We started sharing the mundane.
What we were cooking, what shows we were watching, what snacks we had stocked.
It felt normal — domestic, even. But in a way that made everything else feel quieter.

She was doing her thing—working, adjusting to living alone, finding her rhythm over those months.
And I stayed close, present but not overbearing.

We didn't call it love.
We didn't call it anything.
But I started to notice how naturally we operated like a "we."

I cared when she was tired.
I showed up when she needed a boost.
I noticed when her texts got shorter and knew it meant something was off.

There was a comfort in the way we just existed in each other's orbit — not needing a label, but still moving like something that mattered.

At some point, I realized — I'd stopped thinking of her as just someone I was getting to know.
She had become someone I didn't want to go a day without hearing from.

It wasn't fireworks.
It was something quieter — but deeper.

***

I wasn't used to consistency.
Not like this. Not from someone who didn't expect anything in return.

He didn't say much when he dropped things off — just a quick check-in, a smile, sometimes a simple "Rest today."
But it stayed with me longer than any long conversation could have.

When I was too tired to talk, he understood.
When I needed space, he gave it.
And when I forgot to take care of myself, he reminded me — gently, in his own way.

A text saying "Eat something." A doorbell ring with soup waiting outside. A playlist shared just to make me smile.

He didn't force his way into my life. He found the open doors — and stood quietly inside them, never asking for more than I could give.

And somehow, I started needing those little things more than I realized.
The jokes. The updates. The way he'd just check in to see if I made it through the day.

I wasn't falling in love with grand gestures.
I was falling for the way he made everything feel lighter. Safer. Like I didn't have to carry it all alone anymore.

I never said the words. But I felt them, every time he showed up without being asked.

And for the first time in a long time… it felt like home.

The Playlist, Sunrise & Prayer

Some people say love is about the big gestures. But sometimes, love lives in the quietest spaces — the kind filled with music, grief, and the willingness to just sit beside someone when the words fall short.

During a difficult time of my life — when my grandmother was dying — Amira was there.
Not always physically, but emotionally. Fully.
She didn't need to ask a lot of questions.
She just… sent songs. Checked in. Held space.
And I did the same.

We started building a playlist together.
Not on purpose — it just sort of happened.
She'd send me a song that felt like us.
I'd send one back.

It became our love language for over a year.
And one song kept rising to the top.
"Long Blue Light."
That was our song.
Soft. Wistful. Soulful. The kind of song that held you together when life felt like it was unraveling.

There were nights we'd both be home, texting each other from separate rooms, but syncing up a song.
Just listening. Together. Apart. Connected.

And then one morning — I made her dream come true.

She had once told me she dreamed of watching the sunrise over the ocean. Not just a casual idea, but something she always wanted to do.

So, I woke her up before the sun.
Still dark out. Cold. Quiet.

She had no idea where we were going.
I just told her to trust me.
And she did.

We drove in silence to the beach, the car filled with the low hum of music and the sound of her breathing beside me. The road stretched out like it was carrying us somewhere secret, somewhere we weren't supposed to be but couldn't stay away from. When we stepped onto the sand, the world was still asleep, the sky a deep navy blue with the promise of light.

Then it happened. The horizon bled into oranges and pinks, color spilling across the water until it felt like heaven was cracking open just for us. The wind bit at my skin, but all I felt was the weight of her hand in mine, small, certain, steady.

She didn't say a word. Neither did I. Because in that moment, silence wasn't absence — it was fullness. It was us.

I looked over at her and thought, this is what love looks like.
Not always in grand speeches.
Sometimes just in being the person who makes someone's quiet dream come true.

That sunrise wasn't just light.
It was a moment we never forgot.
And to this day, I still can't hear "Long Blue Light"
without thinking of her,
The playlist we built,
And how sometimes, the deepest love lives in silence,
grief, and a song you can only sing once your heart feels
safe.

***

I don't think he ever realized how much that playlist meant to me.
It wasn't just music. It was how he showed me love — without needing to say it.

Some days, I'd send him a song because I didn't know how else to explain what I was feeling.
Something soft, or warm, or aching.
And without fail, he'd send something back that somehow knew exactly where my heart was.

"Long Blue Light"... that one stopped me.
It felt like everything we weren't saying out loud.
Like love in the background. Grief without words. Hope without pressure.

And then that morning — the sunrise.
He didn't tell me where we were going.
Just told me to dress warm and trust him.
And I did. Fully. Without hesitation.

I remember sitting on the cold sand, the chill sinking into my bones while the horizon slowly cracked open. The sky shifted in layers — pink, then orange, then gold spilling across the waves until the whole ocean seemed to breathe light. My fingers ached from the cold, but his hand wrapped around mine was warm, steady, grounding.

No one had ever done something like that for me. Not just the drive. Not just the sunrise. But the knowing. The way he saw past my careful words, past the mask I wore, and brought me here — to beauty, to peace — without me ever asking. He didn't demand anything. He just sat beside me, watching the world bloom, as if that was enough.

And for me, after all those months, in that moment—it was.
He saw me. Completely. And being seen like that felt like forever.

And in that moment — quietly, inwardly —
I prayed.
Not for strength. Not for clarity.
I prayed that this would be forever.
That the silence would stay sweet,
That the love would stay safe,
That we'd somehow make it through everything the world was going to ask of us.

Sometimes, when the world felt too heavy,
He made space for light.
And for that, I loved him.

Part III: The Divide

The Weight

I started rereading our old conversations, wondering if I imagined what we had.
If I made it bigger in my mind than it really was.
But no — it was real. It just wasn't simple anymore.

She became more careful with her words.
I became more careful with mine.
And that's when I knew something had shifted.

Sometimes it was small — like when I'd ask how her day was, and she'd reply, "Fine."
Sometimes it was bigger — like when I'd say, "Miss you," and she'd respond with an emoji instead of words.

We were still "us." But we weren't whole.

There were questions we weren't asking out loud:
Where is this going?
Do our religions matter?
Are we even allowed to want this long-term?

I felt the hesitation every time I looked at her, every time she looked away.
Not because she didn't care — but because caring wasn't the issue.
Reality was.

She was a Muslim. I was a Christian.
And while neither of us made it the center of our relationship at the start… it was always sitting in the background.
Quiet. Patient. Waiting to be confronted.

She told me early on—with calm clarity—that she had boundaries. Even then, she was direct, but I knew nothing about Islam or Muslims. All I had were the images from the news—the negative, the hateful, the scary. But that didn't make sense, because she was the opposite. She was all love, and more.

"I'm Muslim. No intimacy before marriage. No kissing. We can hold hands, hug, but that's it.
I can only marry a Muslim man.
You'd have to convert.
And I wouldn't be able to introduce you to my parents unless I knew we were getting engaged."

It was all new to me—getting to know a woman without intimacy or the usual norms. She wasn't inexperienced either; she'd been engaged before. And although I insisted on meeting her parents, that never happened with me.
Still, we were living under the rules—an unspoken system that said love alone wouldn't be enough unless every box was checked.

I respected her. I never tried to push past her lines.
But they were there — always.
Looming between the warmth and the weight of us.

We never had "the full talk."
We had moments where we'd try, hint, test the edges, pull back.

We weren't lying.
We were protecting something too fragile to expose.

But the truth?
Avoiding it didn't save us.
It only made the fall feel quieter — and heavier.

I still brought her flowers—sometimes for no reason, except that I loved her. She still kissed my cheek before I left, soft and familiar, like muscle memory that hadn't forgotten us.

And the laughter — it never dimmed. It spilled out of us loud and reckless, echoing off the walls until we were doubled over, wiping tears from our faces, gasping for air. Those moments felt untouchable, proof that whatever else was crumbling, the core of us still knew how to find joy.

***

I used to replay our messages too. I'd scroll back late at night, eyes burning in the glow of the screen, rereading every "good morning", every little joke, every care package tracked by a single line of text: It's on your doorstep. I wasn't just looking at words — I was hunting for proof that what we had was real, that I hadn't imagined it.

We spent every Thursday and Sunday together—sometimes other days too, but those were ours. Then, a year in, something shifted. I felt it in the way I edited myself before hitting send, erasing words that felt too heavy, too honest. I felt it in the way his questions grew softer, more careful, as if he was afraid to ask what he really wanted to know. The truth was, I was afraid too afraid of what might happen if I admitted how much I needed him. Afraid of what it would mean to want someone I could never fully have.

I started editing myself. Holding things in. Not because I wanted to lie — but because I was scared that the truth would undo everything.

He'd ask if I was okay, and I'd say, "Fine." I wasn't. But I didn't know how to explain the guilt that crept in when things felt too good.

I knew where this was going. I also knew where it couldn't.

My path was drawn in permanent ink — rules, family, expectations. I had lines I wasn't allowed to cross.

And still... I crossed them—emotionally, spiritually. I gave him pieces of myself I wasn't supposed to give, and I don't know if he'll ever fully understand that—or what he truly means to me.

I told myself: it's just a friendship. Just care. Just help. But my heart knew better.

When he'd bring up his faith — casually, gently — I'd freeze. Because I didn't want to lose him. But I also knew what my world required.

We weren't dishonest. Just quiet. Careful.

I didn't want him to feel like a project — someone I needed to change.

And he never made me feel like I had to be anything else, either.

That's what made it so painful.

We loved with boundaries. With disclaimers. With limits we never agreed on, but both obeyed.

And that silence between us? It wasn't distance.

It was fear.

Fear that the closer we got to the talk, the closer we came to goodbye.

Space Between Us

It didn't crash down — it leaked in slowly, like water seeping under a door.
One month we were texting constantly, trading jokes and little updates like we couldn't stand the quiet between us. The next month, something had changed. The thread was still there, but thinner, like someone had turned down the volume.

It wasn't cold. Just… less.
Her replies came slower. My thumbs hovered over the keyboard too long, typing and deleting, overthinking every word before pressing send. I'd watch the three dots appear and disappear on my screen — her almost saying something, then pulling back. That hesitation sat in my chest like a stone.

We still cared. I knew it. She knew it. But the air between us felt crowded, heavy with everything we weren't saying. Something had shifted, and neither of us had the courage to name it.

There was never a dramatic argument.
But I could feel myself pulling back, just a little.
Less "good mornings." More "sorry I missed this" hours later.

At first, I told myself it was just life. Work. Stress.
But deep down, I knew what it really was.

Faith.

And while that never seemed to matter when things were light and new, it started to matter more once the idea of long-term began to feel real.

She'd reference her family in passing — how they'd expect certain things.
How being with someone outside her religion wasn't just hard, but almost impossible.
I didn't want to push, so I softened my words.
Held back my questions, even when they felt heavy in my chest.

There were moments I tried to close the gap — texting more, checking in, showing up.
And sometimes, she met me there.
Other times… she pulled back.

It wasn't rejection. It was restraint.
She was guarding something — her peace, her upbringing, maybe even her heart.
And I was trying to hold us together without making it feel like pressure.

One night, I asked if I could stop by.
She didn't say no, but she didn't say yes either.
That hesitation hit harder than a no.

We were still "us." Still something.
But it was wrapped in questions neither of us could answer.

What do we do with this connection when the world around us says it shouldn't work?

Can you love someone fully and still let them go for the sake of peace?

I didn't know.
And I don't think she did either.

But the space between us was growing.

And we both felt it — even in the quiet.

***

There was a point when I noticed he started texting me differently.
The messages weren't shorter, but they felt... measured. More careful. Like he was trying not to say too much — or trying to say the right thing, instead of just saying what was real.
I noticed. But I didn't bring it up.
Because I was doing the same thing.

I had drawn my line from the very beginning. Those rules were never in question. They were etched into me like permanent ink.

But the feelings? Those were new. And they terrified me.
I found myself softening when I read his name on my screen. My chest tightened when hours went by without a reply. I caught myself smiling at things he said long after the conversation ended.

And then came the fear. Not of him — but of myself. Of what it meant to feel this much for someone I wasn't supposed to keep. Every message felt like walking a line, every laugh like a step closer to the edge of something I couldn't undo.

So, I pulled back just a little.
Not because I didn't care.
But because I cared too much.

I kept thinking: I've already told him my rules.
I've already told him what I can't compromise on.
So if he's still here… does that mean he's okay with it?
Or is he staying because he doesn't want to lose me — even though this will hurt us later?

The truth is, I started to worry.
Not just about him. About me.
About how long I could hold on to something that felt this good,
knowing how hard it would eventually get.

So, I said less.
Not out of distance.
But out of protection.
Because it was already starting to feel like love — and I wasn't sure love was going to be enough.

Almost Forever

We didn't walk away without trying.

Before the distance…
Before the silence…
There was effort.
Real effort.

This relationship was different for me.
But somehow… it was beautiful.
To know her as a woman — without physical intimacy —
was something I'd never experienced before.
It stripped away the distractions.
Made space for deeper understanding.

When we met, I didn't know much about Islam — not really. The words "faith" and "boundaries" were just ideas to me, abstract until I saw how deeply they lived inside her. But I wanted to know. Not to debate. Not to prove her wrong. Just to understand.

I read through the Quran.
Not because I was planning to convert, but because I wanted to understand.
Her world. Her beliefs. Her values.
I met with Muslims, asked questions, had long talks about what it would look like — not just to be with her, but to be a Muslim.

She didn't ask me to do any of it.
But I did it anyway.
Because I wanted to see if I could find peace in her world.

She did the same.
She came to church with me.
Watched Christian movies.

Listened quietly as I explained what the resurrection meant, and who Jesus Christ is.

We didn't fight about faith.
We explored it — side by side.
Respectfully. Openly.
Both of us hoping maybe it would feel easier the more we tried.

But the more we tried, the more we learned the truth we didn't want to face. Faith isn't something you borrow for a weekend or slip on like new clothes. It's marrow. It's bone. It shapes how you stand, how you breathe, how you imagine forever.

And neither of us could trade that away — not for love, not for each other.

There were moments we wished we could.
Moments where we held hands and quietly hoped the other would say:
"I'm ready to convert."
But neither of us ever said those words.
Because neither of us ever felt them — not fully. Not honestly.

And that's what made it harder.
Not that we didn't love each other — but that we did, and still couldn't bend on this.

In the end, we weren't choosing religion over each other.
We were choosing peace.
Spiritual peace.

And as much as we both tried…
Our peace couldn't live in the same place.

We never had a breakup.
No big fight. No screaming match. No ultimatums.
Just… less.
Fewer messages. Shorter responses.
But always: Good Morning. and Goodnight, Sleep Well.

We still had our date nights every Thursday and Sunday for over a year.
Still sent each other photos of food, or little updates like:

"Just got home. Long day."
"Thinking of you."
"Sleep well."

But there was a hesitation — wide enough to feel, too vague to define.
I'd reach out.
She'd respond.
But I could feel her holding something back.
And deep down, I knew I was doing the same.

We had created something gentle. Sacred.
It wasn't built on lust or drama or chaos.
It was built on comfort.
Kindness.
Quiet intimacy.

But as time passed, I started wanting more.
I wanted to take our relationship to the next level.
But I wasn't converting — and neither was she.

I was afraid to bring up the religion talk.
Afraid to lose her.
And I know she was afraid too.

There were moments I tried to pull us closer —
Like when I offered to meet her parents.
To show them I was respectful.
That I was serious about their daughter.
That I could be the right man for her.

It just never happened.
But I kept showing up.
Reminding her I was still here.
Still all in.

And she did the same.
She appreciated it.
I know she did.

She was choosing me.
But I wasn't choosing her religion.
And I couldn't bring myself to end things —
Because I already knew: I loved her.

It wasn't that she didn't love me.
It was that she couldn't love me out loud.
Not the way I needed to be loved —
Fully. Openly. Completely.

We were almost everything.
Almost real.
Almost ready.
Almost forever.

But the truth is… almost doesn't build a life.
It builds a memory.

And that's what we became.
A memory.

The kind you don't regret.
The kind you don't delete.
The kind that lives inside a simple phrase:
"It could've been everything."

***

He opened the Quran.
I'd see the faint marks he left in the margins, his pen pressing a little too hard on words he was trying to hold onto. During Ramadan, he fasted with me. Not out of obligation, not out of performance — just quietly, faithfully, even when his stomach growled and his eyes grew heavy.

On my holiday, he celebrated. He didn't just show up — he asked questions that mattered. Not surface-level curiosity, but the kind of questions that made me feel like my faith wasn't a wall between us, but a language he was trying to learn. He didn't debate. He didn't push. He just listened. And in a world where I was so used to defending myself, that listening felt like love.

I knew from the beginning what the rules were.
What my family expected.
What my religion required.
But somewhere along the way, I thought… maybe love could make room for us anyway.

I went to church with him.
Watched his face as he prayed.
Felt the weight of his faith, and how deeply it meant something to him.

We were both trying — not pretending, but hoping.
Still, I felt like we were climbing two different mountains and hoping they'd meet at the top.

When he asked to meet my parents, my heart broke a little.
Because I wanted to say yes.
But I knew what that would mean.
And I wasn't ready to ask my parents to bend for something I wasn't sure I could hold together.

We were trying so hard.
So faithfully.
And still, we were stuck in that space where love lived — but not the kind that could grow.

Some nights I prayed for a sign.
Other nights, I prayed I could make peace with letting go.
But we never said goodbye.
We just... became less.
And even now, I still wonder:
What if love had been enough?

Part IV: The Ending

What If

We didn't just love each other.
We built ideas.
Futures.
Plans.

We talked about marriage.
Not someday. Not in theory.
But in real, practical ways.

What kind of wedding we'd want — low-key, intimate.
Not wasteful. Not performative.
Just something meaningful. Just us and the people who mattered.

We talked about how we'd live together — and laughed at how perfect it'd be.
We were both OCD-clean. Loved structure. Loved quiet spaces and intentional messes — the kind you make while cooking together or rearranging furniture at 10PM because "something feels off."

We talked about raising kids.
What we'd teach them.
What kind of home we'd build — full of warmth and honesty and weird playlists we made on lazy Sundays.

We aligned on so much.

How we'd parent.
How we'd budget.
Where we'd travel.
Even the kind of fridge we'd need.

And in those conversations — those gentle, hopeful moments — I really believed we could make it.

That love and compatibility and respect would be enough.

But faith…
Faith didn't feel like something we could bend.

And the more we imagined our life,
The more we started to realize —
We could build almost everything.

But not the part that mattered most to each of us, in silence, in prayer, in the depth of our beliefs.

Still, I don't regret those talks.
I cherish them.

Because for a moment, we weren't just falling in love.
We were imagining the rest of our lives — together.

***

We'd talk late into the night about the most ordinary things — couches, colors, how many kids we'd want.
And every time, it felt more possible. More real.

I let myself picture it. Our home, sunlight pouring across clean floors and coffee cups half-empty on the counter. Mornings would be quiet, but not lonely — the kind of quiet that feels like belonging.

I pictured our children — their small hands folded for prayer on Fridays, their voices learning hymns on Sundays. I saw them moving easily between both worlds, not confused, but whole. Running from church pews to mosque rugs, learning that love doesn't erase difference, it embraces it. I imagined their laughter filling our home, proof that we had built something strong enough to hold both faiths without breaking.

I used to say I never wanted a big wedding.
Too much pressure. Too much performance.
But with him… I imagined one anyway.
Not for show.
Just for us. Something beautiful, honest, sacred.

He would've made a great father.
Patient. Present.
The kind who reads bedtime stories without skipping pages, who teaches kindness by example.

And we dreamed of it all.
Not as fantasy — but as a life we almost believed could exist.

Loving You Was Not Enough

It had been over a year.
A full year of trying.
Of holding space.
Of waiting for things to shift.

I kept thinking maybe if I just stayed steady — if I kept showing up — she'd feel safe enough to meet me where I was.

We still checked in.
Still met up.
Still said good morning and sleep well, good night.

Sometimes we would talk for hours — thoughtful conversations, playful texts, little moments that reminded me why I loved her.
Other times, there was nothing until the next day.

And it wasn't because we didn't care.
I know we did.
It was because we couldn't figure out a pathway forward.

I felt it in the space between texts.
In how hard I was trying to keep things from slipping.
In the way she thanked me more than she asked for me.
Gratitude started replacing affection.
Quiet distance replaced closeness.
I told myself: This is just a phase.
People get busy. Things slow down and pick back up.
But deep down, I knew this wasn't temporary.

I knew what it looked like when someone was trying.
And I knew what it felt like when someone had let go—
quietly, respectfully, without wanting to hurt you.

That's what I did too.
I let go with grace.
I didn't make it messy.
It just started to happen, without ever saying the words.

We had spent a year circling the same walls.
Trying to merge two worlds.
And as much as I respected her boundaries and wanted to believe love would be enough — It doesn't erase faith, culture, fear, or family expectations.
It doesn't always get to win.

She gave me her soul.
I gave her mine.
And I don't blame her for any of it.
But I do miss her.

Even now, I can't tell you exactly when it ended.
It just… stopped growing.
And when love stops growing, it quietly starts fading.

She still lives in my phone.
Not just in messages — in moments.
Moments I haven't deleted.
Moments I probably never will.

Sometimes I scroll back to our first few texts, my thumb moving slow, as if rushing might erase them.

Then there are the ones buried deeper.
The ones that stop my breath.

"You're my most perfect partner."

I stare at those words until they blur.
Until the screen fades.

Until all I can feel is the ache of knowing love that perfect still wasn't enough to keep her.

I meant that.
And I know it.

But life doesn't bend for the perfect partner.
It bends for timing. For circumstances. For the path that feels safest.

She chose peace.
I chose her.
And in the end, I guess that made all the difference.

And still, if you asked me who taught me how to love differently —
more gently,
more patiently,
more wholly —
I'd say she did.

***

There were still moments that felt like us.
But deep down, I was afraid.
Not of him—
but of what it would mean to love him fully.
To choose him openly.
To walk into a life I had never seen modeled, never been taught was possible.

He was willing to compromise.
To meet in the middle.
He never asked me to leave my religion.
He pictured a life with both—
both holidays, both traditions,
children who knew both churches and mosques,
who chose faith with full exposure and love.

But for us, that meant letting him lead.
And I couldn't see myself surrendering that, even in love.

I didn't want to lead him on.
But I couldn't let go either.
So I stayed—somewhere in between.

He sent long, winding messages—his whole heart poured out in paragraphs.
I'd reread them until my chest ached.
And then shrink my reply into something small. "Okay. Thank you. Goodnight."
Not because I didn't love him.
I did.
But love had rules in my world.
Rules I couldn't break.

From the start, I was clear about my faith, my family.
Those boundaries never shifted.
And still… he stayed.

He met me where I was, again and again.
But I couldn't meet him there.

Letting go wasn't a single break.
It was a slow unraveling.
I stopped sending good morning first.
Stopped asking about his day at night.
Swallowed the affection pressing at my ribs until silence was all that passed between us.
What we had—reduced to threads in my hands.

And yet, I still scrolled our old messages.
"Sleep well. Be safe. I miss you."
Little digital proof we once believed in us.
I traced the words on the screen like touching them might conjure him back.

He never said too much.
He just showed up.
With care. With patience.
Like I could be held without being asked to change.
Like I could exhale.

But I couldn't give him what he needed.
Not without betraying the parts of me I'd been taught to protect.
Faith. Family. Fear.

And I did love him.
That's what made it all so hard.

Some nights, the sunrise plays in my mind.
The way he woke me in the dark. "Trust me."
The silent drive, the empty roads, just us.
The cold sand under my shoes.
The horizon cracking open, spilling fire across the water.
His hand finding mine.
Silence between us that felt like safety.

That's the version of us I keep.
Not the doubts.
Not the rules.
The light.
The moment I believed forever was possible.

People assume that if you walk away, you didn't care.
But I cared.
So much it broke me.
I prayed for peace.
For another ending.
But not every love is meant to stay.
Some are meant to shift you.
Open you.
Show you what's possible.

He was never my mistake.
He was my awakening.
My mirror.
My safest space.

Still him.
Even now.
Always.

.
.
.

Until the silence shattered.
My phone lit up, his name burning across the screen.
Every voice in my head screamed to let it go dark.
But my hand was already moving.

Because some love doesn't fade.
It waits.
It fights.
And when it calls—
you either answer,
or you lose it forever.

Summary

In the end, it wasn't a lack of love that ended. It was two people standing at a spiritual crossroads — hearts aligned, but faith pulling them in different directions.

Their final exchange wasn't about blame, anger, or regret. It was about respect. It was about heartbreak that came from trying everything, and still having no way forward without compromising core beliefs.

One expressed love and understanding.
The other, in return, revealed the depth of their pain and inability to walk away — a truth that made their choice even heavier. They both cried.
They both knew.
And they let go — not because they wanted to…
But because holding on meant betraying the very values that once brought them closer.

What remained was sorrow, honesty, and the kind of love that's too deep to forget — but too impossible to sustain.

Author Bio

Jason Alan is a chef-turned-entrepreneur, real estate broker, owner, investor, and now first-time author.

From the heat of professional kitchens and the food & beverage industry to leading in business and earning recognition as the #1 CENTURY 21 real estate agent for two years, his journey has been anything but ordinary. Along the way, he skipped his final year of high school, graduated early from university, backpacked through Europe, lived abroad in Belize while starting and running a business, and developed a deep love for culture, food, and the stories of people everywhere.

Grounded in family and faith, Jason has always carried a creative side, and now he brings that to the page. With *Loving Someone Is Not Enough*, he shares a story meant to open hearts through love rather than close them with assumptions—an invitation to see others with LOVE, even when they are different from ourselves.

www.ingramcontent.com/pod-product-compliance
Lightning Source LLC
LaVergne TN
LVHW090536110826
845146LV00003B/1119

* 9 7 9 8 2 1 8 8 3 0 9 2 2 *